LET'S GO!
BOATS

by Tessa Kenan

TABLE OF CONTENTS

Boats **2**

Words to Know **16**

Index **16**

South Huntington Public Library
145 Pidgeon Hill Road
Huntington Station, NY 11746

tadpole books

BOATS

Boats float.

water

They help us move on water.

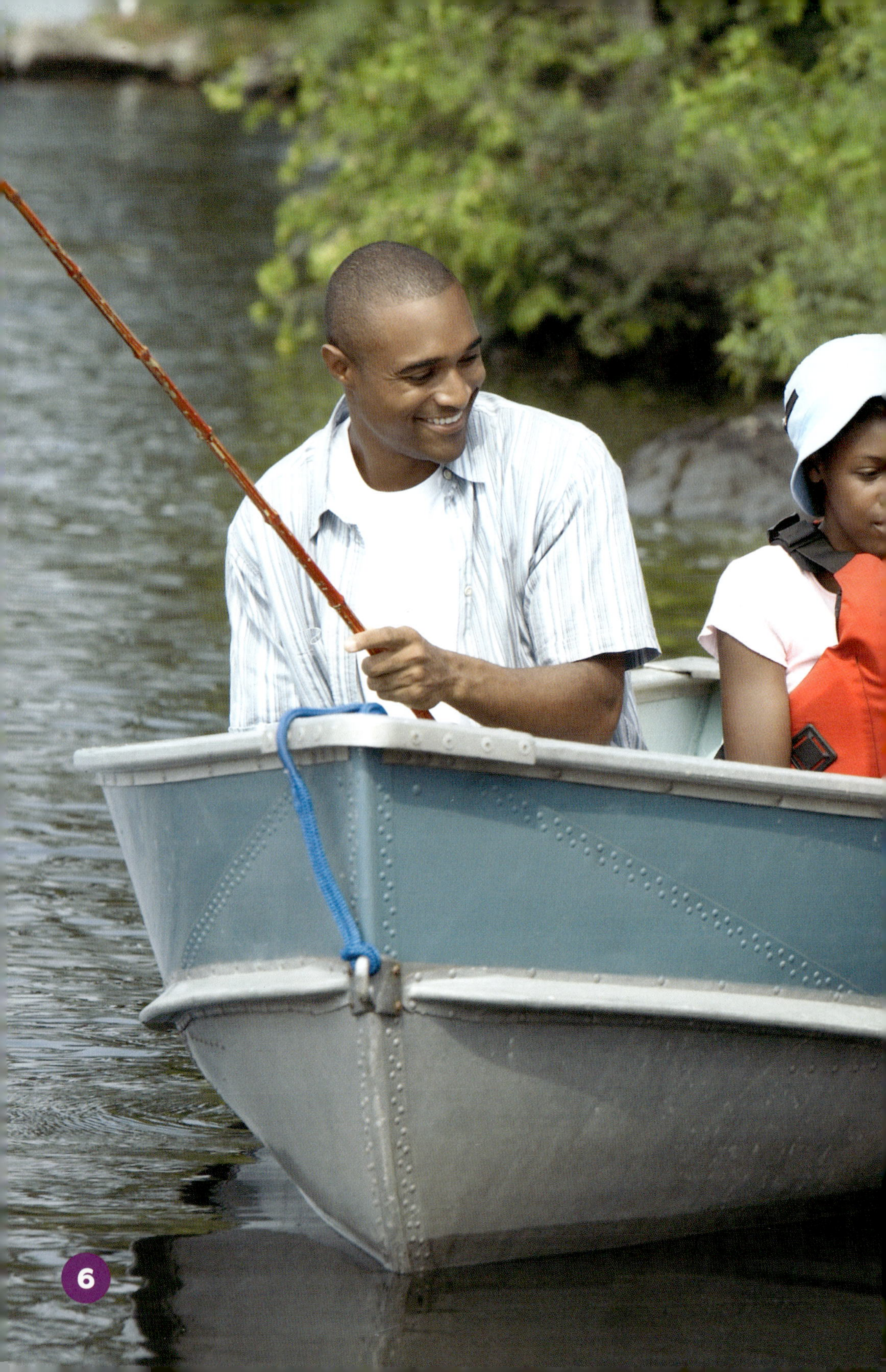

fish

They help us fish.

8

They help us travel.

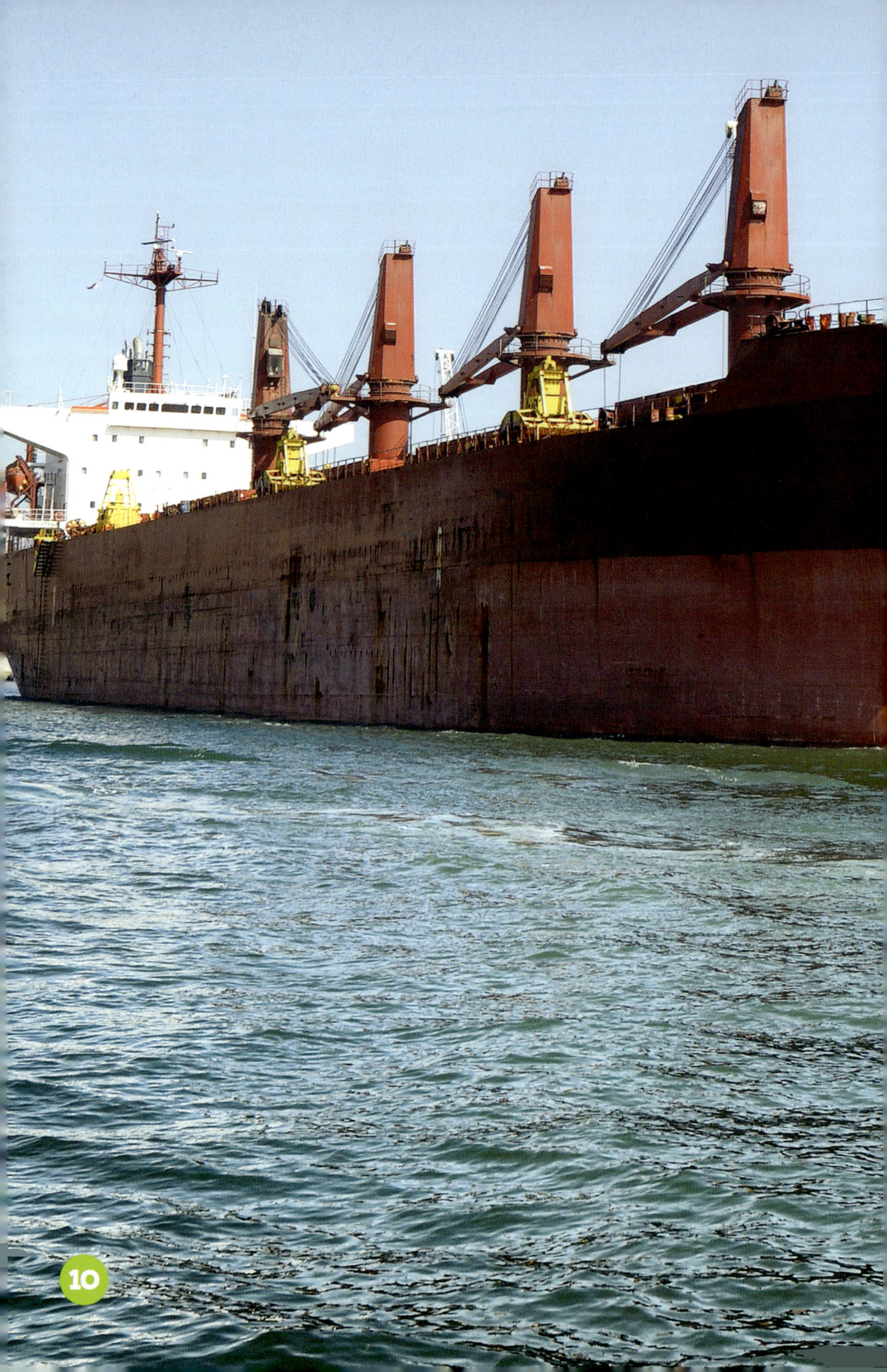

They help us pull.

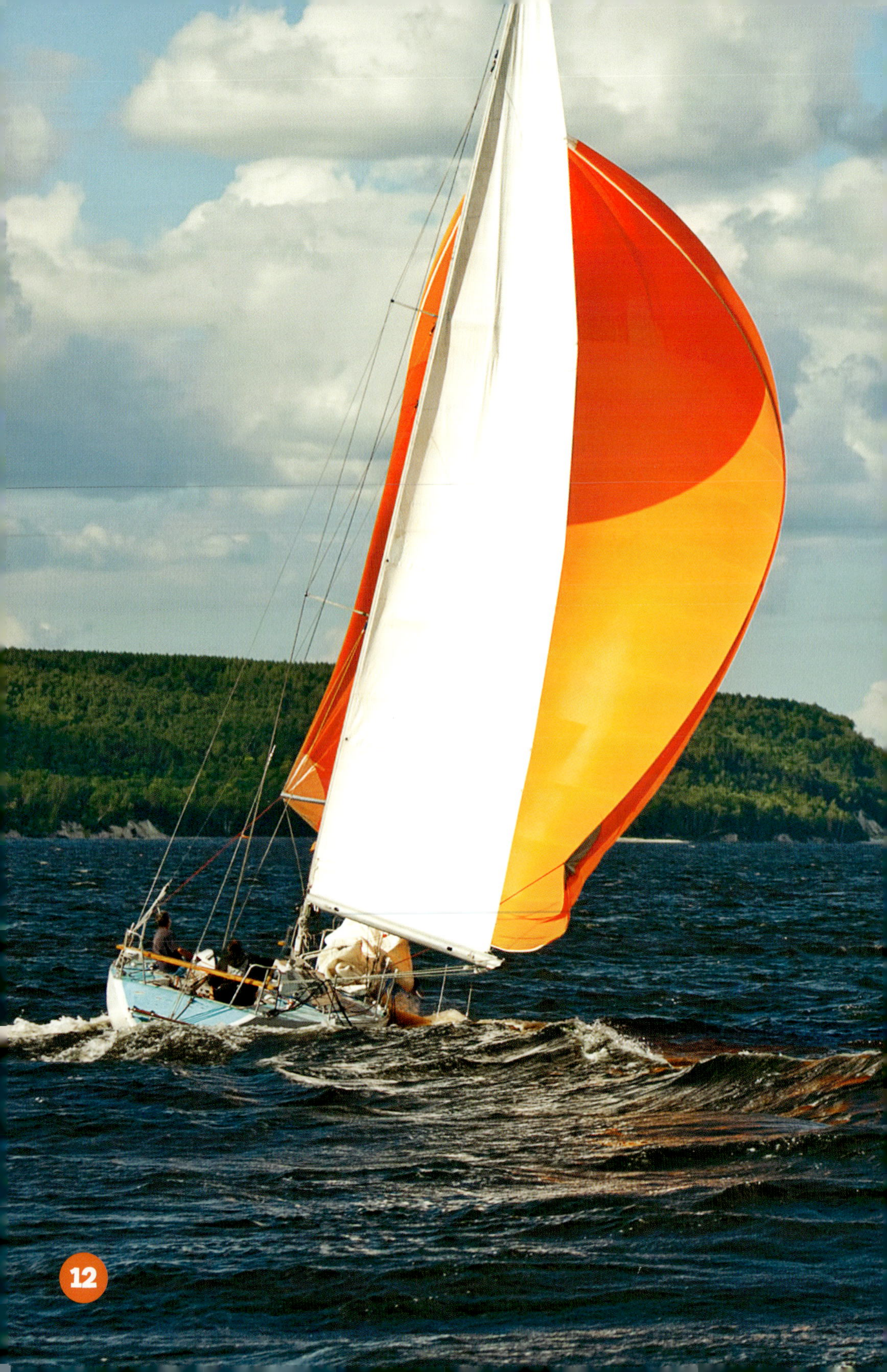

They help us sail.

They help us have fun!

WORDS TO KNOW

fish

float

move

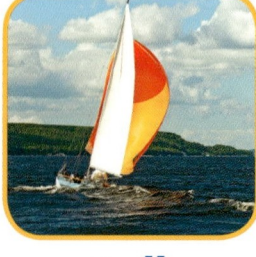

pull

sail

travel

INDEX

fish 7
float 3
move 5

pull 11
sail 13
travel 9